This Walker book belongs to:

_____

_____

First published 1992 by Walker Books Ltd
87 Vauxhall Walk, London SE11 5HJ

This edition published 2011

2 4 6 8 10 9 7 5 3 1

This book has been typeset in Garamond Light Educational

Printed in China

British Library Cataloguing in Publication Data:
a catalogue record for this book is available from the British Library

ISBN 978-1-4063-3814-0

www.walker.co.uk

TOM AND PIPPO
ON THE BEACH

Helen Oxenbury

WALKER BOOKS
AND SUBSIDIARIES

LONDON · BOSTON · SYDNEY · AUCKLAND

One day Daddy
and I went to the
beach in the car …

and of course Pippo
came as well.

Daddy said that the sun was really bright and I ought to wear my hat, because the sun might make me sick.

I said that it didn't seem
bright to me and I didn't
feel sick and anyway Pippo
needed to wear my hat.

Daddy said he would make a hat for Pippo so that I could wear my hat. He said he would make Pippo a hat out of newspaper.

I said to Daddy,
"Look, Pippo doesn't
like the paper hat."

"I know! I'll wear
it and he can
wear mine."

I'm glad Pippo's
got the best hat,
so he won't feel
sick in the sun.